THE ATLANTIC

THE PACIFIC

For Emmersyn, Olivia, and Grace
Curious Crows Books | An imprint of Curious Crows Media LLC

Curious Crows Books

First Edition 2023
Library of Congress Control Number: 2023945180
Paperback Cover ISBN: 9798850411077

Visit us online at www.curiouscrowsmedia.com and serenedreamsart.wixsite.com/carolineberkey
Follow on Instagram @tylerjlabelle, @whatmakesmyhomemyhome, and @serene.dreams

What Makes My Home, MY HOME

Written by
Tyler and Jordan
LaBelle

Illustrated by
Caroline Berkey

Be back soon!

I showed them all sorts of fun and wonderful things. Sofia loved the rodeos. Gila drank gallons of sweet tea and ate BBQ, gumbo, and pecan pies. Wren sang along to the bluegrass, jazz, and country music.

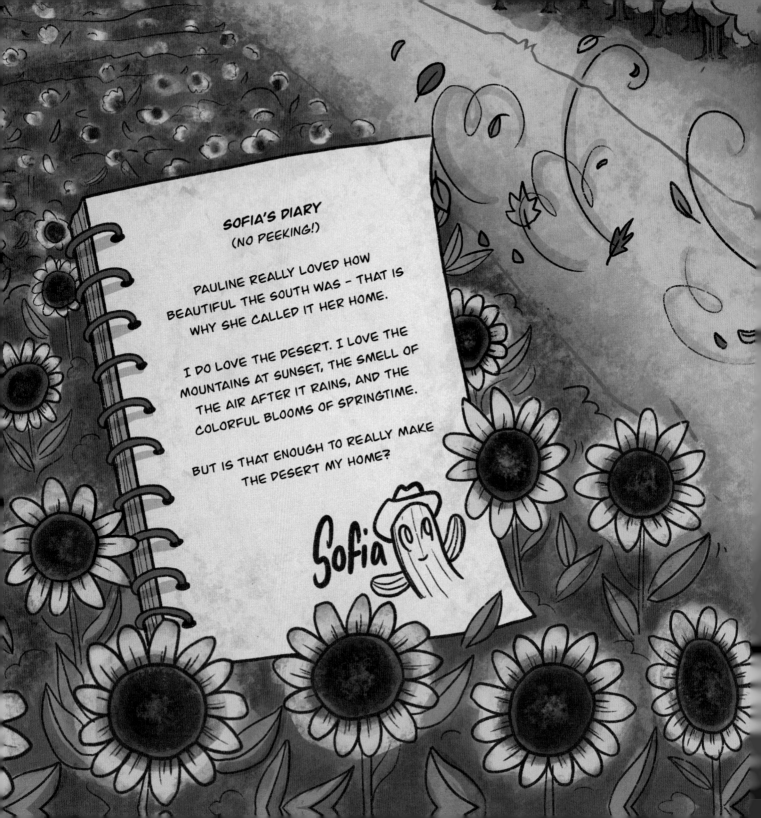

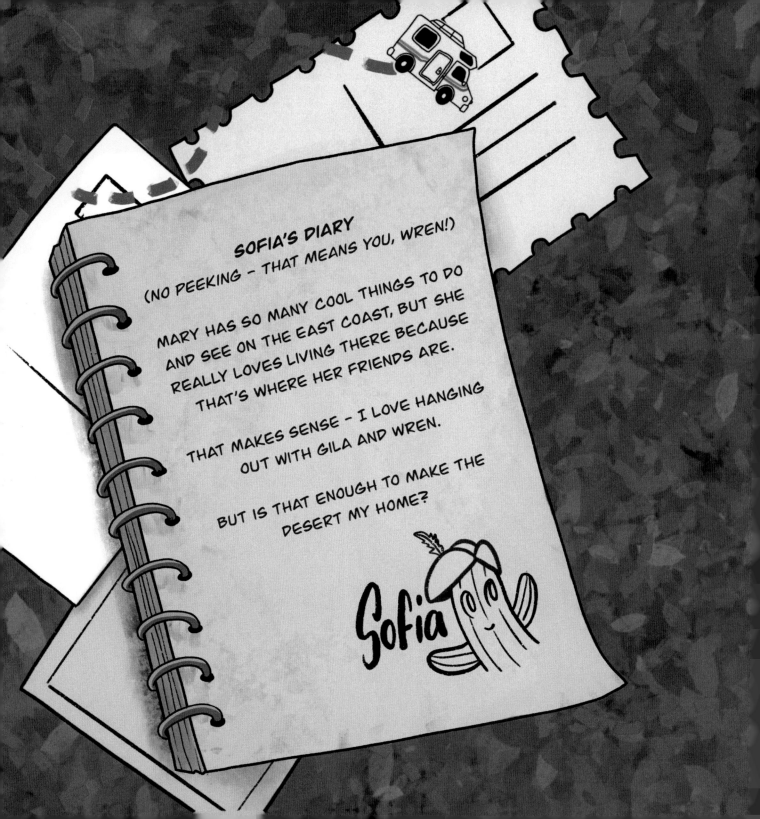

Tyler LaBelle

Tyler LaBelle is a small business owner living in Tucson, AZ. After reading countless books to his three young girls, he was inspired to create a fun story with a meaningful theme that celebrates the desert and encourages children to be proud of their homes.

Jordan LaBelle

Jordan LaBelle, a professional copywriter with over a decade of experience, has always had a passion for stories. While in college, he studied literature in both Ireland and at Oxford University. In his free time, he writes a variety of fiction, including a novel titled *The Bridgeman Dossier* that can be found on Amazon.

Caroline Berkey

Caroline Berkey is an illustrator originally from Caracas, Venezuela. They moved to Tucson to study at the University of Arizona and fell in love with the Southwest. Their passion for visual storytelling grew from a fondness of comics, animation, and children's books.

Made in the USA
Coppell, TX
01 December 2023

25086964R00024